PRAISE FOR JESSICA DRAKE-THOMAS

Jessica Drake-Thomas has a wealth of knowledge of things you've only tasted in shadows. In this collection of gothic poetry, she opens her palms to let some of these dark whispers free into the night –the freedom of a shared language etching itself into the history of the world, to become legend. As things do when they die and are buried. If you've ever heard the begging of the blood moon, pulling you from slumber to tiptoe through the darkness...if you've ever gnashed your teeth at a lover's neck...you will find wisps of your own darkness among these pages. With dark, romantic language, vengeful love spells, and the ghosts of old Salem wandering lost among the brittle paper, Burials is a haunting your soul won't soon forget.

— MELA BLUST, AUTHOR OF *SKELETON PARADE*

T0265948

Burials is at times fierce and at others keening, but most often it is both at once. Jessica Drake-Thomas writes macabre love poems with the dazzlingly morbid whimsy of a young Morticia Addams driving her "hearse in seafoam green," seeking her Gomez in this sad, lonely world. "I have learned that / love is cheap here, / and something is important / about the idea of // a nice girl," she tells us. But for the witch-hearted girl, Drake-Thomas gives us love spells that offer a kind of healing for the haunted, for the many ways love so often fails us.

— LINDSAY LUSBY, AUTHOR OF
CATECHESIS, A POSTPASTORAL

Good writing relies as much on resonance of imagery as words, and the best writing, as is the case with *Burials* by Jessica Drake-Thomas, circumvents traditional connotations of imagery and imbues it with new and magical meanings. Early in this poetry collection, Drake-Thomas establishes the images of buried women in her poem *Queen of Sticks*, "Meet my lover the executioner. He kills people for his bread." This collection is a mass grave teeming with lovers as executioners, and the bodies left like corpses in their wake.

The cadavers are domestic and down-trodden — the house-woman" whose "mouth became a door, a large round hello for anyone to walk in. And everyone did." They are true crime victims — Bella, a body confined to a *Wych Elm* and allows her to remember her tongue — but then asks "who listens to a pile of bones?" They are masochistic — as the speaker of *Pocketfuls* pondering her love for her own love /executioner, "Aside from that maybe I do — love you like Ophelia loves the water she floats in."

Burials is, in fact, a poetic exhumation of bodies interred, in trees, caskets and homes, used and forgotten like the still-living speaker in "White Silk Lined Coffin." Its narrator's breaths keep time with our own gasps as we realize she is both entombed and cognizant of the "cool black beads are slipping between your fingers and the prayers your silent lips form are only for you." The book is a skeletal secret whispered into the fleshy ears of the living in an eloquent elegy by Drake-Thomas to disposable bodies lifted from the hurt and the dirt with which they have too long been covered.

— KRISTIN GARTH, AUTHOR OF *FLUTTER: SOUTHERN GOTHIC FEVER DREAM* AND *CANDY CIGARETTE: WOMANCHILD NOIR*

BURIALS

JESSICA DRAKE- THOMAS

CLASH

Copyright © 2020 by Jessica Drake- Thomas

Cover by Olivia Croom

CLASH Books

clashbooks.com

All rights reserved.

No part of this book may be reproduced in any form or by any electronic or mechanical means, including information storage and retrieval systems, without written permission from the author, except for the use of brief quotations in a book review.

M.

"I am writing to you as an act of immolation, relief."

— —ALLISON BENIS WHITE, *PLEASE BURY ME IN THIS*

CONTENTS

QUEEN OF STICKS

This is the Witches' place.
All that remains
is the line of oak poles,
spaced evenly,
blackened
by use.

Above is the sound of the stars —
bells and breaking glass.

This is where
we come to die.

I am the Queen of Sticks.
This is where
my gods answer me.

I have been here before.
My flesh was warm.

It crackled
and broke.

I screamed,
my throat bursting open.
I awoke—

One stick, I hold in my hand,
smoothed by daily use.

Another awaits me,
long ago, later on—
backlit by a sunset,
black.

Sticks, stones
break bones.
lies kill people.

Meet my lover,
the executioner.
He kills people
for his bread.

He chews. Swallows.
Complains that it tastes
of ash mixed with blood.
Once, he bit down
on a rusted nail
dropped in the dough.

He thinks it's
a curse
from the dead.

Every day, he gets up
to burn witches.
He doesn't know
or see

the woman
in front of him —

Only a body.

LOVE SPELL NUMBER ONE

If you love someone
who does not love you back,
try this spell.
You'll need three strands
of his hair.
All good love spells
require someone to
give something
in order to
get something back.

Do this on the night
of the new moon.
The darkness signifies
new beginnings, hope.

Light a candle—
a red one, of course.
Bring something copper—
a shiny new penny.
Hold the coin
in the palm of your hand
as you light the candle

and burn each blond hair.
As the strand frizzles away,
much like his patience
for your mental instability
and your constant texting,
close your eyes.

Imagine his indifference
disappearing.
Imagine replacing it
with passion.
Imagine his eyes, his smile.
Think of the last thing
he said to you.
The old jokes. Your demeanor.
After your breakdown,
things just aren't the same
anymore. It's not your fault,
but…

Open your eyes. There
should be no "but."

THE HOUSE-WOMAN

When the pain came,
I folded into myself
like a Peruvian mummy,
my arms holding
my folded knees
to my breast.
My toes became roots,
digging down deep
into the ground,
my spine, a curved staircase.
The halls of my arms
became gray, stiff
as driftwood.
My hair was a knotty curtain
covering my face.

In time, I grew hollow — I became a house.

Like all houses,
I was a shelter, inhabitable.
My mouth became a door,
a large, round Hello
for anyone to walk in.

6

And everyone did,
floorboards slamming beneath
dancing feet,
echoes of early morning
late night conversations,
sloppy with
spilled drinks,
messy with smoke, and
music that I hated.

Soon, they were gone.

I was haunted.
Anyone who's lonely
contains ghosts—

empty after

the world has been
stained with love
and full of voices.

The ache returned.

I searched and found:

Once-colorful wallpaper,
faded yellow flowers.
The drapes, choked with dust.
Decaying carpets.
Distilled light
came in through
my eyes, broken windows.

BANSHEE

I.

When I woke, it was dark.
I could hear
nothing.
I could see
nothing.
Just shadow and gray light,
filled with the scent of smoke,
bruised petals,
sick, sweet.

My limbs locked in paralysis,
wrapped in the embrace
of an iron coffin.

I called out:

Darling,
I think I'm
burning

from the inside out

8

golden skin splitting, turning to ash,
flakes glittering, swirling on dry, crackling air.

There was nothing,
no response.

II.

Once, I was a small child,
chasing ghost trains in the mist.

The ground, damp beneath my bare feet,
as rain slipped down
the blue leaves of the hyacinths I carried.

In the tree beside me,
hanging from branches like witches' fingers,
frayed ropes and the Nine of Swords danced in the wind.

A man wearing a coat
like the silence behind the stars
stepped around the witch-tree,

shot me in the cheek.

I watched my blood sink into the ground,
death wrapped itself about me,
a winedark stain,

and birds flew out of the tree,
susurrations of wings beating like my slowing pulse.

III.

Here I am, the dead returned
to walk the burned earth,

howling up at the slice of a moon, thin like a knife.

When I woke, I screamed my name into the void
and something ancient answered,

breath scented with grave dirt.

MINE

I want to wear you
like you were mine,
an interwoven design
etched across my back,
over my hips,
which you say
you like so much.

I want to use
you
like you're using
me,
that is,
shamelessly.

I want to pick up
your broken pieces,
set them somewhere
safe, dry.

But I can't fix things —
only break them.
I'm nothing

that you want
to keep.
When you go,
you won't look back.

What I feel for you
is a gray house
in a dream
half-remembered,
a black bird
that flies unseen.
Evidence
of how alone
I am.

There is a
word for this
you don't deserve.
I should keep it,
not gifting it to you
in this way —

tracing it with
my fingertip
on your wrist.

TWO GHOSTS

"Here we left it," she said. And he added, "Oh, but here, too!" It's upstairs," she murmured. "And in the garden," he whispered. "Quietly," they said, "Or we shall wake them."

–Virginia Woolf

You are
the blue moon over the desert,
the dark glove in the snowstorm,
waving goodbye.
This isn't a love story.
This is how we fail
each other.
This is how
we don't stay friends.
Commit, ensnare, possess—
words we run from.
Broken, devour, caress—
words you can keep.
What I want—
to lay out my bones
next to yours,

linger along tiled hallways,
rough with dust.
watch in silence
as the stars dance,
a slow fade.
But you have nothing
to give,
your face turning away
into the light.

THE POISONING

My pulse is in my ears
as I wait for the man
they call
dark horse
black bird
ill omen.
And my stomach —
beneath my clasped hands,
it aches. My liver
has died inside of me
after a night of too much
white wine
vodka tonic
gin blossoms
in ulcerous bursts
ripping through my stomach lining
in a bright arterial spray.
My sadness is a poison,
my greatest strength,
and a soft cloak,
a knife stuck in my ribs.
Today, I wished that I
didn't know you.

Today, I realized
how happy I am
that you're here.
I had so much
to tell you,
but won't.
I'm always speaking
through a spirit board,
and you've thrown away
the planchette.
My invisible fingers
circle the word GOODBYE.
He nears—
black dog
dark bird
bad omen—
he's nothing
but a murky silhouette,
the scent of wine, woodsmoke.
I tell him what
I want—
I want to drive a hearse
in seafoam green,
I want a bright sword
to stab at bouncy castles,
I want a carousel horse
trimmed in mistletoe and mirrors
and I want a necklace
made of the teeth
of my friends,
so I can keep their bones close
against this pulse
at my throat.
This want,
this needing—
It keeps me up at night.
He nods, yes—

his smile is pointed,
his eyes burn.
You shall have this
and this
and so much more.
His antlers are trimmed in stars
and he wears a soft, grey mantle.
His mossy nails click
on age-clouded glass.
He hands me the blood-red bottle.
I drink,
belladonna salting my lips,
burning all of the way
down.
As my core howls,
the world spins,
fading,
to a dark, empty
sea
where
the stars
burn
out.

POCKETFUL

You promised that
I wouldn't be alone tonight.
Even though
we both know:
a trip to the psych ward
is a turnoff, and
only the person
you pretend to be
would care enough
to stay.

We sit out on the balcony, after
you bring me home.

I can feel the space
between us —
like two blue lips
forced open,
sucking in
silt-stained water.

You ask me if
I'm still "hung up on you."

You spit out the words —
I'm an annoyance,
grit at the bottom
of the glass
you drink from.
You ask me if
I love you.
I laugh and say no.

Although,
I get chest pains when
you tell me
about everyone that
you sleep with.
To you,
I'm a dead woman —
a bad ghost,
sticking around
after you've already
disposed of my corpse.
To your disappointment,
I return with the current,
floating up from
my water-marked grave.

"Do you still want to go
to your formal with me?" I ask
your silhouette.
No one has ever invited me to one —
I've always been
the girl that
everyone hides because
they can't fix me —
I'm not a paper to be edited.
A problem to be solved.
A doll to be dressed.
But I pretend to be.

"Of course," you say.
"I found a dress," I tell you,
eager to please.
"Is it pretty?" The moon glints
off your glasses.
"Yes."

We go inside where
you get in my bed,
turn away.
I wrap my arm around you,
the small spoon.
I watch the
back of your neck,
fish-pale in the dark.
You sleep, I think.
I lay awake, haunted
by the dead river daughters,
writhing in the corners
mouths gaping like O's,
and the contents of my pockets,
brown and dry, fragments
which stick
beneath my fingernails.

The worst part is,
and I can't stop thinking —
I don't want
this.

When I bought my dress
for your formal, the saleswoman
was more excited than I was.
To be honest, she chose it.
My smile felt full of dirt, and
a rope of blackened laurels
twisted around my throat.

In the mirror,
my lips turned blue.
I touched the material
that clung to my ribcage —
dark as the night sky,
whisper-soft.
It made my waist look tiny,
and the skirt twirled just so.
It's the kind of thing one wears
to please a man
who cannot want her
as she is.

Every hope I had
that you gave me
is fingerworn smooth
and nestles in my pockets —
round black stones
that weigh my body down.
The steel-cold water
licks at my toes.
A fish surfaces for air.
I do not step in.

I don't know
why I'm not
letting you go.

Aside from that maybe
I do —

love you

like Ophelia loves
the water she floats in.
It's full of
light and detritus,

her bright red hair
and the blue tulle tendrils
of her torn dress
and an ink-cold shadow
that promises to
take her places.
Her chest heaves
as she inhales,
accepting the water
as it is.

She twirls,
her eyes stare,
as if seeing the water
for the first time
and the fish all come up
from the dark
to kiss
the rotten flowers
that fall from
her outstretched hands.

A KIND OF DYING

A bright light is at
the place where
the doors of dark pine
fail to meet.

There is movement on the other side.

In the gloom of the Owls' Club,
my eyes adjust
to find him
in the crowded bar,
walking toward me.

My glass is filled with
a dark liquid,
occult medicine,
syrupy with apricot.

I have learned that
love is cheap here,
and something is important
about the idea of

a nice girl.

I meet her everywhere
in his diary
with its broken pages.
He hunts her.

She can't be
real.

My hands are covered in dust.

I smell a kind of dying.
It's here. He's here, too,
coming closer.

This cipher of a man,
this scentless apprentice,
he keeps his secrets.

So I rifle his pages.

He's working on
a collection of perfect specimens.

Briefly, his gaze fell on me.
And I wanted to be

his

kept in a glass casket,
treasured. A single fingerprint
smudging the surface.

Or so I thought. But no longer.

Standing behind me,
he runs his fingers
through my red hair.
His lips
travel my skin.

I want
to be lost
in the cold night
of his eyes
as my breaths
pause.

I open my eyes.
He's no more than
a bad ghost.

You and I are so alike, I say.

His face darkens
as he turns away —
a sudden dance step.
He's moving,
looking,
spinning.
His hands
reaching out
to other women,
whose bodies
are drawn to his,
gray moths to a black light,
birds chattering with a joy
unknown to either of us.

I sit still. Waiting.
Dressed in black silk,

back arched,
pale hand falling
out of a reach,
watching the movement
in the light at the space
between the doors.

I am not free, like you.
I call out,
broken open like a shot bird.

He returns,
slamming me
in the back of the skull.
With a blunt object, flashing
like a hungry fish rising
from the murky depths
of a pond.

I have no time to feel

fear —

only love.

My sight dims,
the dark doors open.

He wraps my body
in fat-soaked silks
to leech away the desire
pouring from my being.

Through means known
to him only,
he bottles it

and carries the cut glass
in the pocket on his chest —
a trophy
as he walks on farther shores.

LOVE SPELL NUMBER THREE

If you love someone who
is using you for your body,
try this spell.
You'll need paper,
a pen, and a blue candle.
All unrequited love spells
use a blue candle.
Write his name
on the paper.
Draw a waning moon
beneath his name.
Fold the paper
into a small square,
envision your feelings
for him
entombed within.

Do this on a Friday,
so you can ignore
his late-night, drunken
booty calls
all weekend.
Do this sky-clad,

so you can use
your energy and spite
to cleanse your body.

Let the candle wax melt
over the paper. Fold it
into a small casket.

Bury this
in your garden,
beneath the compost heap.

Draw a bath.
Hot as you can
stand.
Let the hurt
leave your body
like steam rising
from the surface.

BELLA AND THE WYCH-ELM

Based on the occurrences in Hagley Wood in 1943.

Four boys found her
on a Sunday morning
playing King Arthur's court.
Lancelot hit the tree with
a stick-sword,
her jaw fell out
of a crack in the old elm-tree,
its trunk squat and ancient.
Her weathered skull,
a bird's nest still firmly
tucked like a crown
within her brunette hair,
tumbled out next,
clunking grimly
on the ground
beside the scattered bones
of her left hand.

Gawain screamed,

and the King turned pale,
while Lancelot and Perceval
turned and ran.

The words, like wildfire, began to appear
on the schoolyard's brick wall,
and the dumpster behind the grocery store,
emblazoned across the hermit's house
(he might have done it himself
sometime in the night),
the Wychbury church's sign, and
the cemetery's lone obelisk
in white chalk:

Who put Bella in the Wych Elm?
Who put
Bella
in the witch-tree?

The bones and flesh of the tree
have enveloped Bella,
fingers closing in a fist.

Bella? Who put you here?
Speak. Will you
speak?

Her jawbone detached,
hanging,
mouth a slack-jawed scream
as her teeth fall out,
the faded taffeta
knotted
behind her chin
the only bit
left holding it in

lets

go

of its secrets.

In the gloom,
a dry whisper,
as green wick twigs
sprout
from her pug-like nose
and weeds blossom
from her eye

socket.

I don't want anyone
to see me like this.

There's a nakedness —
an honesty found only in death,
that the living can't respect.

I can't speak for myself,
so they all speak of me,
breath from their lungs,
dust from the chalk.

I can see it again — the cycle
where people start
to fail me.

Then silence as

woman becomes tree,
tree becomes woman
woman becomes skeleton

skeleton
becomes
bones
ponderous
and alone.

Until the police come

and wrestle her from
the grave
to poke and pry
apart what's left.
Try to piece together
a woman, a corpse
that's already
half-dust,
a few navy-blue striped rags
with the tags
cut out,
peach taffeta underthings,
battered shoes,
a fake wedding ring,
and silence.

Who put
Bella
here?

Rumors ebb and die.

Bella sits in a box
at the morgue,
dreaming of the shelter
of trees
and a winter morning
when the stars faded.

I remember, she says
to no one, for
who listens
to a pile of bones?

I remember when
I had two lips,
a tongue. Skin.
Breasts, thighs.
To do lists, long drives,
wine, warm blankets.
I, too, experienced
hunger, desire.
I had a voice.

OUTSIDER

It's just my curse
to stand still
while everyone else
moves on.

To hang out
in dark corners.
Make things
go bump
in the night.
Watch
the living
as they sleep.
Envious.
Alone.

To wander, crying
down the hall
until he
comes awake
with a start.

I hold out my hand

when he looks at me —
eyes wide, mouth askew.
I think I could love him,
with all my dark little heart,
his warm fingertips
pass through me,
always
failing to connect
because
I'm not whole, and
he sees me
as something
long defunct
who'll never leave
a warm impression
in his sheets,
vanishing
with the click
of a lamp.

THE HAUNTING

We lived in a house
with an angry ghost.
The house was
dilapidated, paint peeling.
We were married.
In this life,
that would never happen

because I
cannot handle
any versions of myself
that are not my own,
and this version of me
that you've created,
weak and wanting,
cannot exist.

I painted it,
the dream-house, in
egg-yolk yellow.
Knitted a knotty blanket —
I made it a home,
a nest of sunshine

and soft wool.

The paint peeled,
crackling away from
the walls and the siding
to reveal the grey,
broken wood beneath.
The ghost hated
the yellow.

One night, we made spaghetti
that we never finished.
The ghost showed me
his true face.
It was his home,
where the walls
oozed black mold,
the foundations
sunken.

You wrapped
your arm around me,
led me out
like the house was
falling in, on fire.

We drove around the city,
and this was my city,
strange and unknowable.

I can't help but think,
as I sit in a dry bathtub
at three in the morning,
dressed in my clothes —
how in this story, awake,
I have no hometown, and
you're the one

who must leave.

While I want some
version of you,
your facade, perhaps,
I don't need this
hidden you,
the one who
malingers.

WHITE SILK-LINED CASKET

Dirt rained down on the lid,
drumming like
an afternoon rain,
a steady tap
of fingers,
slowly subsiding
in their urgency.

I don't know
who dug this grave.
It must have been me.
My hands are mud-caked
as I clasp them over my chest.
I'm alone now
with the one thing
I had feared: silence.

When you left,
you did not wrap
a red string
around my finger.
Now,
there is

no bell to tell
those at the surface
that I'm down here,
still breathing.

This wasn't how I wanted
to go out—
no roaring funeral fire,
juniper branches catching,
my skin popping and burning like stars.

Instead, my hands brush against
this soft fabric.
This lush, cold darkness.

I curl up into myself
because I know
right now,
cool black beads are
slipping between your fingers
and the prayers
your silent lips form
are only for you.

REASONS WHY I HAD THAT MELTDOWN LAST FALL, OR I THINK YOU MIGHT BE A NARCISSIST

It's not for any one
reason, but many.
Certainly not anything
anyone else has done,
like telling the truth, or making
a mapwork of bruises
across my skin.
Not because of
my illness or the hurt
I fight to keep bottled
behind a Resting Bitch glare
and closed mouth.
Not because sometimes that pain
comes out, a swarm of bees
from a kicked hive,
and I become a nasty woman,
powerful in my rage,
burning your city and all of your
bridges, napalming your rivers.
Not because of any one thing, but
it's all coming together
in one place,
tucked beneath my sternum

beating hysterically—
a ship going down,
a building falling,
a fist unclenching,
pierced through by
four iron-dark arrows.

You
held me skewered
by a promise I kept
at my expense.

One which you
broke.

CHANGELING

When she picked me up
out of the lace bassinette,
how was she to know
that her blonde-haired blue-eyed child
with the milk-soft skin was gone,
slipped away silently
in the light of a sickle moon
beneath the crust of the Hill.

All her life she knew
hearthstones,
heated by warm fires
Sunday church, handbags, pearls.
Family dinners where
the worst thing
was slipping spinach
into your napkin.
What she knew,
in the world above:
happy endings mean marriage
and chubby, wide-eyed children.
What she learned:
marriage clutches and binds,

and children can grow up
to become demons,
wrapped in flesh.

All I know are unharvested stones,
the moon's light on my heathen skin,
wild green eyes, pointed teeth,
tiny fairy feet pattering the paths
in places where
sometimes the heroine
falls in love with a peasant girl,
changes her mind
and runs off with a man,
who she abandons in the forest.

We've always battled.
Clothes, pronunciation, standards,
how to make mashed potatoes.
I bring spite and snake oil.
She, her iron-bound will.
She fights for dominance —
she wants me to fit
in narrow shoes.
I fight for freedom —
my return to the Hill.
I look at her, sitting across from me
at a table set with cookie tins
and shattered porcelain.
We both carry old wounds,
scars that run deep.

I wish that I could give her
her sweet child back.
The one who slumbers
beneath the Hill
where thorns bloom
and wraiths dance.

KINDRED

In fifth grade art class,
I had to draw a mimic
of Kahlo's *La Venadita*.
I was a bougie blonde girl
wearing scrunchies,
eating white bread sandwiches,
reading fluffy fantasy paperbacks.
What did I know of pain?
I scribbled it hastily in
my sketchbook
with a hot pink glitter gel pen
because I didn't like her —
I didn't understand
the pain portrayed.
As with most things,
she takes living to appreciate.

I hated the colors.
Always felt nauseated by
the drab grays and browns
of the nine-tree forest around her,
the queasy blue and sick-stain yellow

of the storm's face,
the bright crimson of her blood,
oozing but not
spackling the leaves of
the broken branch beneath
her hooves.

Nine arrows —
five in the back,
shot by surprise,
four in the heart,
shot while looking deep
in the shooter's eyes.

It's overkill,
but *La Venaðita*,
she floats, never
falling, and
I wish I knew —
the secret to being graceful
under enemy fire,
the crown of her antlers
rising above her.

At twenty-nine, I know
what Frida Kahlo meant
when she portrayed
herself as a deer
with a woman's head,
her deer body
pierced through by
long arrows.

La Venaðita isn't even
here, at the museum,
but a glossy-paged poster

is on sale at
the gift shop for fifteen dollars,
and there's a matching mug,
in chunky ceramic, too.

I reach up,
touch her glossy, printed cheek,
think about how
she's smiling like
she knows something —
and this I know, too.
How it feels to live
when everything hurts.
How to look at other people,
see how they are
unbroken, blind.

There is both
something ugly
and something beautiful
about chronic pain
and falling in love
with the drab colors
of your own body.

I remember a diary entry
of Kahlo's:
I hope the exit is joyful —
my smile so real,
the flash of that last daylight
on my teeth, brilliant
as my back arches
and my body is broken open,
so everyone can finally see
all of the brutal crimson,
and I hope never to return.

I walk out of the museum,
arrows protruding
from my back and my chest.

US HEATHENS

A found poem from Robert Hicks's *A Separate Country*

My heart pounds,
drumming down the seconds.
I try a kind of cantrip
from my long-ago childhood,
edited, for precision is key:

Pray for us heathens
now and at the hour of his death
in the room
packed to the ceiling
with bootleg whiskey
and killing powder.

We are two hunched,
black-clothed
figures, creeping
up the back staircase.
Le Monstre is splashed across
the dirty wall in red wax,
a slanting, feminine cursive,
bleeding out

down the wall.
This place is still, abandoned.
He turns back to me
and I know to keep
silent.

This is where
the dying were kept.
Well-swept floors.
The beds, stripped.
An astringent scent
lingers.
He steps across
the gleaming floors —
the man that they call
black horse
dark bird
ill omen.
His teeth are stained,
his skin is pale,
smells of sandalwood.
His back is straight,
shoulders strong.
I hear his whisper —
a cry.
Someone who will not be heard
on this earth again.
I pull the knife
from his back.
I open my arms,
let him slip to the ground,
blood spackling his lips,
surprise in his eyes,
two pools where fish
rise up from the dark.
He tells me to go,
so he can die alone.

Outside,
a hearse drives down
Saint Charles Avenue.
Soot from the wrought-iron balcony
comes off on my hands,
but I feel clean
like someone who's got
a second chance.
I turn
to see a *precise line*
of blood, marking my trail.

I must hurry.

I put him deep in the grave,
beneath a great tree,
burying his killing knives,
fanned across his chest,
like a snake,
deprived of his bite.

Death is the province
of the sacred feminine.
To lead all by the hand
on their way to
decompose in the dark.
Work that is
ugly and raw.
Man's cult of beauty,
a discarded corset
in the ashes of witch-fire.

As I finish laying the dirt,
I remember him:

The demon on his black horse,
fire-eyed and mutilated

above an open grave,
a human abattoir,
the spoils of a thousand souls,

while I stood in a circle of witches.
We were strong women,
faces round as the moon.
We chanted: *Mama,*
pray for us heathens,
and planned the hour of his death.

FAMINE AS A LOVER

He arrives beneath a storm-sick sky,
a grotesque Godiva,
he rides a rusted out motorcycle,
a weary horse
with socket eyes.

His long hair
rattles like wind through dry wheat.
Threadbare jacket
creaks, its denim worn.
Converse soles crunch gravel.
His tattoos have
all been blacked out.

He looks like a Skarsgård.
His flask is full
of nepenthe.

His hands, his jaw—
you love their shape.

Famine lures you with
his devil-may-care stare,

(beware the deadlights)
the soothing sound of his voice

He knows all of the right
things to say and do.

I'm in shining armor (a cold fish).
Baby doll. Pretty lady.
(are you buying
this?) *I think I'm falling for you,*
Manic Pixie. Dream girl.
I want to give you (a violent end)
the world. All of me.

His prerogatives are
your long bones, the heat stored
beneath your skin.

His chest cavity is a gaping pit,
filled with absence.

No matter what he puts into it—
it's never satiated.

You're a distraction.
Another chance for him to prove
there are no exceptions.

Kiss his bee-stung lips—see the stars crackle
beneath your eyelids.

Feel his thin fingers grasp.
You're dying—he's
putting hand
to mouth, sucking marrow
from your femur.

Blood oozes between
the filed points of his teeth.

He feasts on your flesh, masticating
like pale fire and dry moths,
eats his blood-damp napkin.

When he leaves, there is

a field of trampled dirt,
a husk, face down.

THE BLACK DAHLIA RUMINATES

you broke my body
open, baring my secret crimson
and left
just as the soft down

and (i rose) to your caress
which rendered me ugly, wanting
i felt so alone
just as the soft down

rose to your caress (you were
gone). a door slammed shut.
return my voice

come back (i am)
scraped open, raw (no longer myself, but my death)
(you left me, like you always do)
shattered, blood-soaked
open on the january ground
(for some other good time girl)

eyes like obsidian stones
(pathetic)

JESSICA DRAKE- THOMAS

my traitor lips
grinning
to my ears

THIS IS HOW I BURY YOU

I make a wax version of you,
carve the word
you used against me
in his soft flesh
to make him
become you.
I rub your wounds
with salt.
Whisper the right words,
with intention.

In time, this will devour you.
When you feel my fire,
remember me, smiling.
This hex is a virus blooming,
spreading its dark spoor
into your veins, lungs, life, luck —
dragging you under
where you belong.

This will take everything.
Gnawing away my flesh,
until I am nothing

but bone,
completing the work
that you began.

I hold you over a flame.
Your head curls inward,
melting into
your shoulders,
into your middle,
until you are
nothing.

I take what's left of you —
small drop of wax,
bury it
in cool, dark earth
by a stream
so you
can't find
the way back.

ATROPOS

You must first learn
there is no beginning, no end.
The language, told by knots
in red woolen yarn.

If only reading were simple,
a pendulum poised above a map,
the fall of bones, leaves —

Petals, opening to reveal, in time —
a fully blown rose.

You must learn how
to proceed by touch —
how the yarn is rough against
the pads of your fingers.

Feel, the thick and thin. Read:
hand closed to hide the scar,
of an oath kept, and
never revealed.

A chest rising and falling

beneath pressed sheets.
Slowly, now.
Turn the strands to feel
a different angle —

find more knots, old patterns.
Questions, no answers.

Blind One,
how does it feel
to be immortal? To have power,
but no agency?

There's something beautiful
about attending the mortal end.

Pull out your silver scissors,
make the final cut,
listen: the death rattle.

LOVE SPELL NUMBER TWO

If you love someone
who has left you,
try this spell.
You'll need
an entire bottle
of wine.
Drink this
out of a mug,
an extra large one,
which reads:
I <3 MY DOG.
All good love spells
require libations
to the goddess
that is you.

Do this on the night
of the crescent moon.
The moon, too, is
only a slim piece of herself.
She mourns your loss
with you.

But she, like you,
will either become whole
or reborn again
soon.

There will be
other people.

The moon, like you,
is hungry.

There is another name
for this spell.
It is "To Cure A Bad Habit."
Pull nine hairs
from your own head.
Make sure this hurts,
but only a little.

Wrap the hairs
around a nail.
Hammer the nail
into a wall.

Your pain will
go away when
the nail rusts
and your hairs
fall away.

The hole will remain,
but, like a freckle,
you will forget
it is there.

IMBOLC, 2019

Imbolc translates to
in the belly, as in,
a containment.
As in, a dark horse,
belly round with foal
walking through
a snowy field.
Or, my dog,
curled at my feet,
osteosarcoma
blooming
in her femur.
Or, me,
wrapped in
a white coat,
a poem
unspooling
from my mind.
The child of my heart
brings me a stuffed
blueberry that squeaks,
then wants to go for a walk

for the first time in weeks.
I feel grief,
like dry leaves in wind,
stirring, within.

NOTES

QUEEN OF STICKS: Based on the life of Catherine Monvoisin, known as La Voisin. She was a French fortune-teller, poisoner, and sorceress. She was the central figure in L'Affair des Poisons. She had six lovers, one of which was an executioner.

The Vampire LeStat by Anne Rice, p.47: "It had been years and years since I'd walked in the witches' place. The moon was bright enough, as he'd said, to see the charred stakes in their grim circle and the ground in which nothing grew even one hundred years after the burnings."

LOVE SPELL NUMBER ONE: *The Good Spell Book: Love Charms, Magical Cures, and Other Practical Sorcery* by Gillian Kemp, see the spell on pg.8, "To Strengthen Attraction."

THE HOUSE-WOMAN: Based on the series of paintings Louise Bourgeois created between 1946 and 1947, called the Femme-Maison paintings, where nude female figures are portrayed with their heads and bodies replaced by architectural drawings, addressing questions of female identity.

A KIND OF DYING: The Owl's Club is a bar in Tucson, located in a former mortuary. The main barroom is lit solely by candles. This piece was written after reading Patrick Süskind's *Perfume: The Story of a Murderer*.

LOVE SPELL NUMBER THREE: *The Good Spell Book:*

Love Charms, Magical Cures, and Other Practical Sorcery by Gillian Kemp, see the spell on pg. 23: "To Get Rid of An Unwanted Lover."

BELLA AND THE WYCH-ELM: In 1943, the skeleton of a woman was found in a tree by a group of young boys. Afterward, graffiti began appearing all around (the town) reading, "Who put Bella in the Wych Elm?" The woman is theorized to be a spy, a prostitute, or even the victim of an occult ritual by gypsies. So far, no one has come forward with any definitive information on her murder. There are also theories that the graffiti artist was her killer.

See also: "Why We Love—And Need To Leave Behind—Dead Girl Stories," by Kristen Martin, published on *LitHub*.

OUTSIDER: Based on *A Ghost Story,* a 2017 David Lowery film.

KINDRED: Frieda Kahlo's last journal entry read: "I hope the exit is joyful ... and I hope never to come back ... Frida."

US HEATHENS: *A Separate Country* by Robert Hicks

THIS IS HOW I BURY YOU: *Burials,* the 2013 AFI album

ATROPOS: Based on Yllish Story Knots from Patrick Rothfuss's *Kingkiller Chronicles,* as well as the Three Fates. Atropos is the one who cuts the threads of life.

LOVE SPELL NUMBER TWO: *The Good Spell Book: Love Charms, Magical Cures, and Other Practical Sorcery* by Gillian Kemp, pg. 38: "To Cure a Bad Habit."

ACKNOWLEDGMENTS

Thanks to Leza and Christoph at CLASH Books for reading my dark little book and calling it lovely. It's been a pleasure to work with you.

I owe an enormous debt to my mother. You always pick up my broken pieces, and have provided me with support while I pursue my passion. I'd be dead fifteen times over without you. Additionally, you've always made reading and writing a priority, and that's definitely made me the writer that I am today.

Additional thanks to the Pink Plastic House Poets and Erin Post for editorial advice on the pieces in this book.
The poems in this book have appeared in:

NewMyths "A Kind of Dying"
*Star*Line* "White, Silk-Lined Casket"
Ghost City Review "Two Ghosts"
Grimoire "Love Spell Number Two"
Anti-Heroin Chic Magazine "Love Spell Number One"
The Rhysling Award Anthology and *Eye to the Telescope* "The Poisoning"

Rose Quartz Magazine "Pocketful"
Mooky Chick "Bella and the Wych Elm"
24 Hour Neon Magazine "Banshee"
Three Drops from a Cauldron "the black dahlia ruminates"
Animal Heart Press "Atropos"

ABOUT THE AUTHOR

Image Credit for Author Photo: Lauren Drake-Thomas

Jessica Drake-Thomas is a poet and fiction writer. She's the author of *Burials*, as well as two other unpublished books. Her work has been featured in *Ploughshares, PVSSYMAGIC, Coffin Bell Journal,* and *Three Drops from a Cauldron*, among others.

ALSO BY CLASH BOOKS

TRAGEDY QUEENS: STORIES INSPIRED BY LANA DEL REY & SYLVIA PLATH
Edited by Leza Cantoral

LIFE OF THE PARTY
Tea Hacic-Vlahovic

BORN TO BE PUBLIC
Greg Mania

NO NAME ATKINS
Jerrod Schwarz

WATERFALL GIRLS
Kimberly White

GIRL LIKE A BOMB
Autumn Christian

CENOTE CITY
Monique Quintana

HEXIS
Charlene Elsby

I'M FROM NOWHERE
Lindsay Lerman

WE PUT THE LIT IN LITERARY

CLASHBOOKS.COM

FOLLOW US

TWITTER
IG
FACEBOOK

@clashbooks

www.ingramcontent.com/pod-product-compliance
Lightning Source LLC
Jackson TN
JSHW080205141224
75386JS00029B/1064